LOOK AND FIND

Tigger

Disney's **Winnie the Pooh**

Cover character illustrated by Sue DiCicco

Illustrated by Animagination, Inc.

Written by Lynne Suesse and Deborah Upton

Published by
Louis Weber, C.E.O.
Publications International, Ltd.
7373 North Cicero Avenue
Lincolnwood, Illinois 60712

www.pubint.com

8 7 6 5 4 3 2 1

ISBN 0-7853-4409-8

Publications International, Ltd.

Look and Find is a registered trademark of Publications International, Ltd.

Manufactured in China.

P9-COO-702

Tigger is having a tiggerific dream that he is in a land of Tigger. Everything is stripedy, just like our lovable buddy! Look through this tiggery scene to see if you recognize your favorite characters and other objects decked out in the cat's pajamas!

Jump Rope

Butterfly

Eeyore's Tail

Kanga

Pooh

Piglet

Owl

Tigger and his friends love to stargaze. The night sky is loaded with so much to see: stars, planets, fireflies, and other silly space stuff. Sometimes they even imagine funny things. Look up in the sky with Tigger, Pooh, Piglet, Roo, and Eeyore to find these starry objects:

Star Pooh Bear

Star Ship

Star Kite

Star Roo

Star Honey Pot

Star Tigger

Star Piglet

Star Eeyore

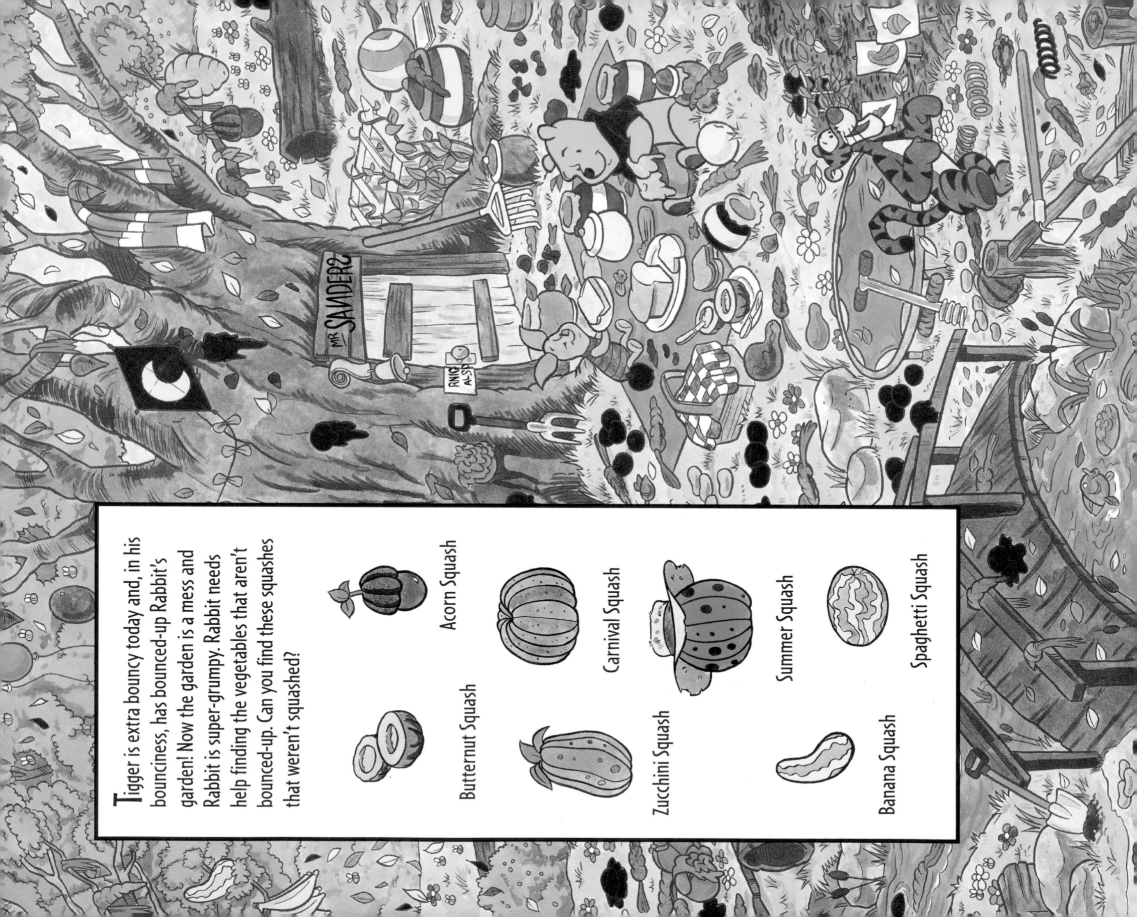

Tigger is extra bouncy today and, in his bounciness, has bounced-up Rabbit's garden! Now the garden is a mess and Rabbit is super-grumpy. Rabbit needs help finding the vegetables that aren't bounced-up. Can you find these squashes that weren't squashed?

Acorn Squash

Butternut Squash

Carnival Squash

Zucchini Squash

Summer Squash

Banana Squash

Spaghetti Squash

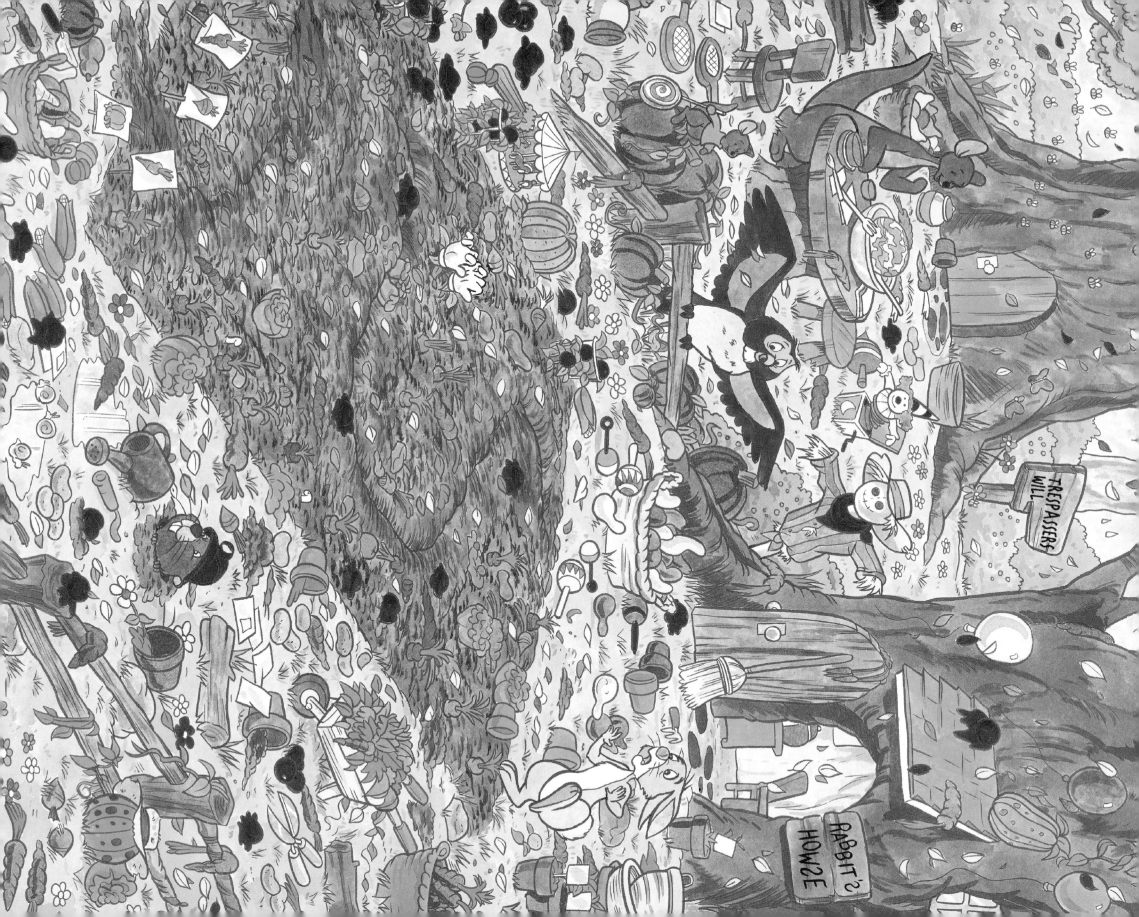

Tigger stops by Owl's house for tea, and Owl shows him his big wall filled with family portraits. Owl has so many family members and friends! Look at all the portraits and help Tigger find the most special friends and relations on Owl's wall of fame.

Grandma Spot

Brother Owllie

Auntie Owlga

Grandpa Feather

Baby Owlivia

Great-Grandma Screech

Uncle Hootie

Cousin Owlen

Christopher Robin takes the gang on a camp out. They sit around a campfire toasting marshmallows while Christopher Robin tells a very scary story about heffalumps and woozles. The gang thinks they hear heffalumps and woozles coming near their campsite, but the noises are really just ordinary things. Find who is making all the scary noises.

Crackle Crackle

Buzz Buzz

Krick Krick

Squeak Squeak

Splish Splash

Croak Croak

Tap-tap-tap

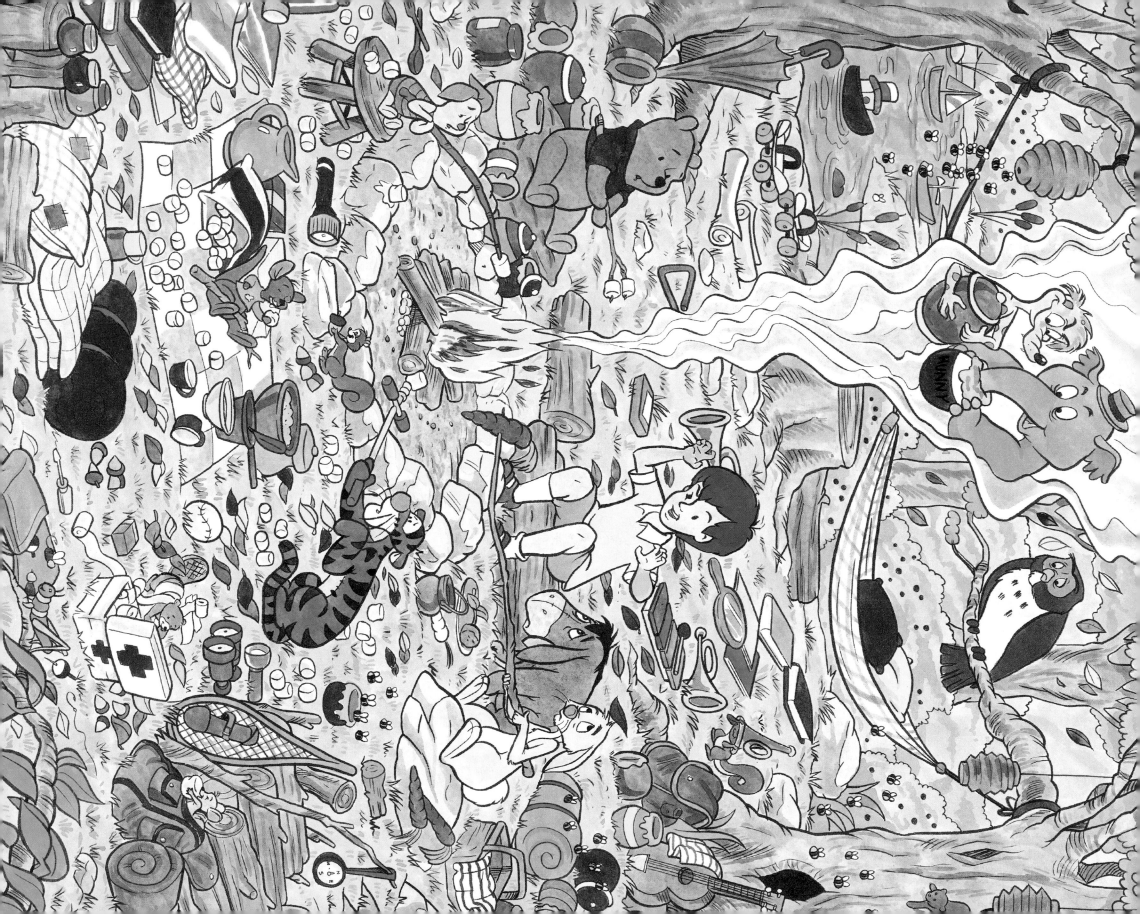

Tigger was trying to surprise his buddy bear Pooh by cleaning his house, but what a mess he has made—Pooh's honey pot collection is all mixed-up! Pooh thanks Tigger, but now he can't find his favorite honey jars. Help Pooh by finding these special jars from his collection:

Rainy-Day Honey Pot

Tea-Time Honey Pot

Bouncing Honey Pot

Winter Honey Pot

Summer Honey Pot

Blustery-Day Honey Pot

Everyday Honey Pot

Full Honey Pot

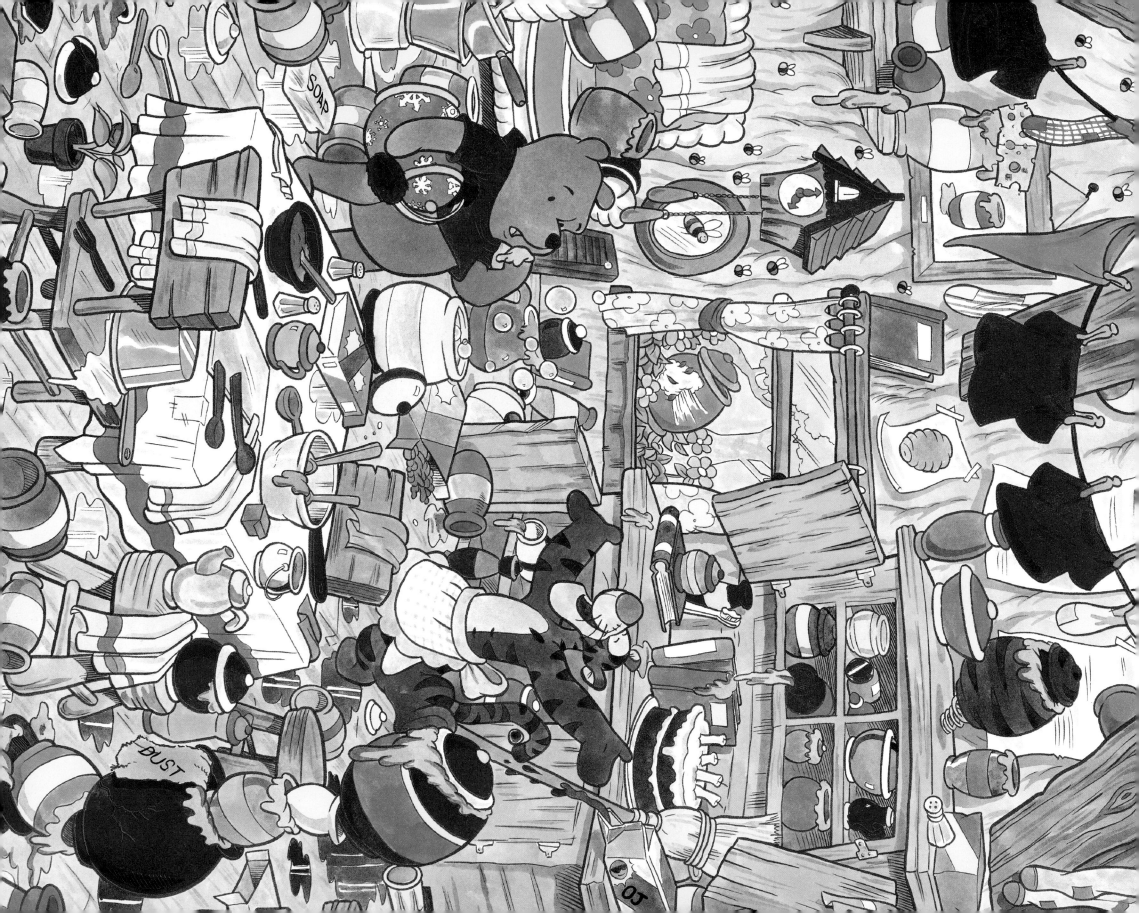

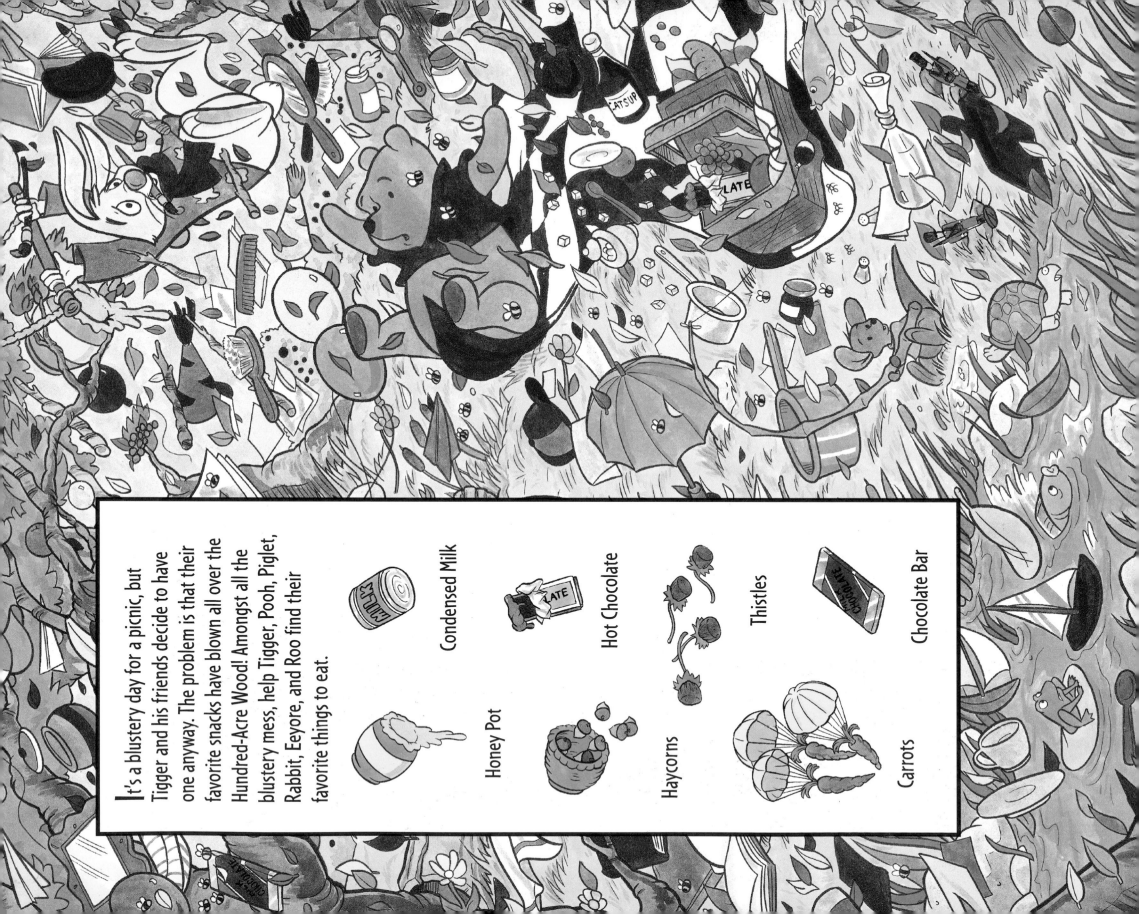

It's a blustery day for a picnic, but Tigger and his friends decide to have one anyway. The problem is that their favorite snacks have blown all over the Hundred-Acre Wood! Amongst all the blustery mess, help Tigger, Pooh, Piglet, Rabbit, Eeyore, and Roo find their favorite things to eat.

Condensed Milk

Hot Chocolate

Thistles

Chocolate Bar

Honey Pot

Haycorns

Carrots

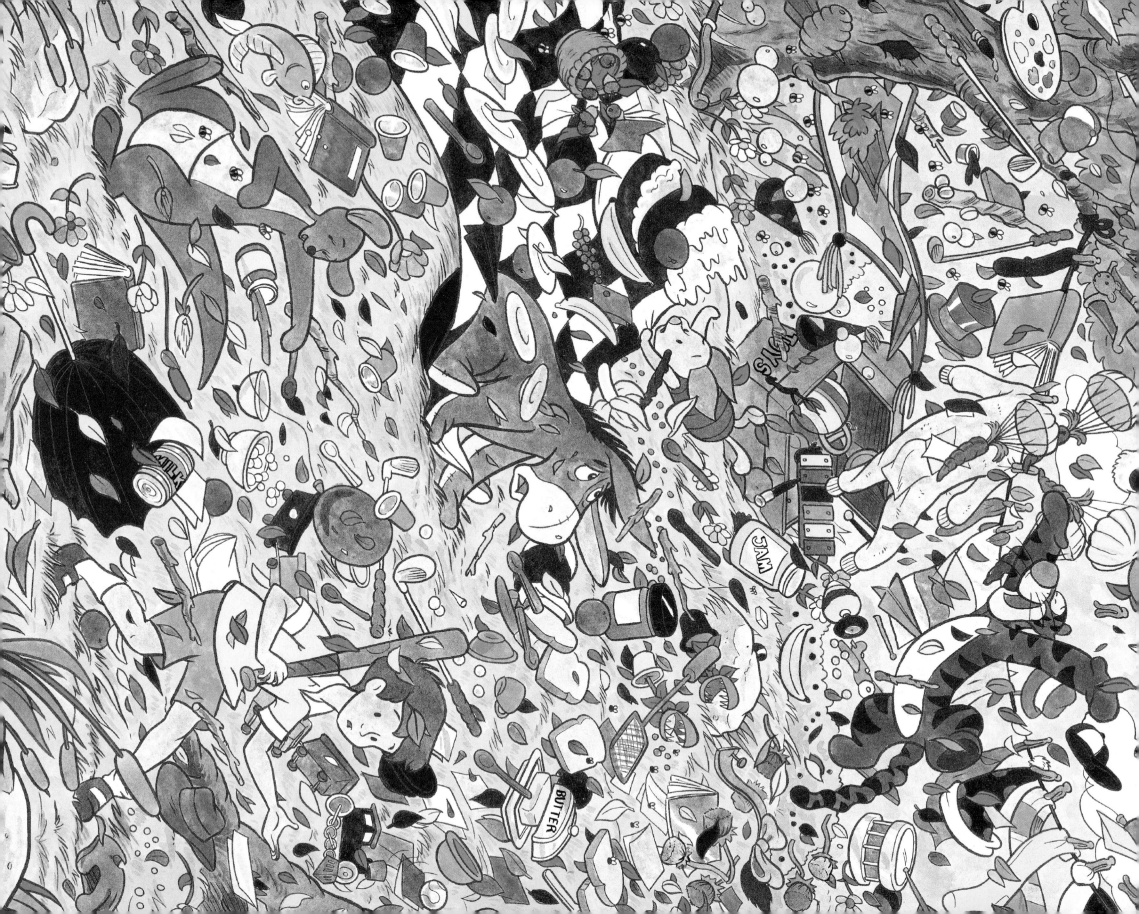

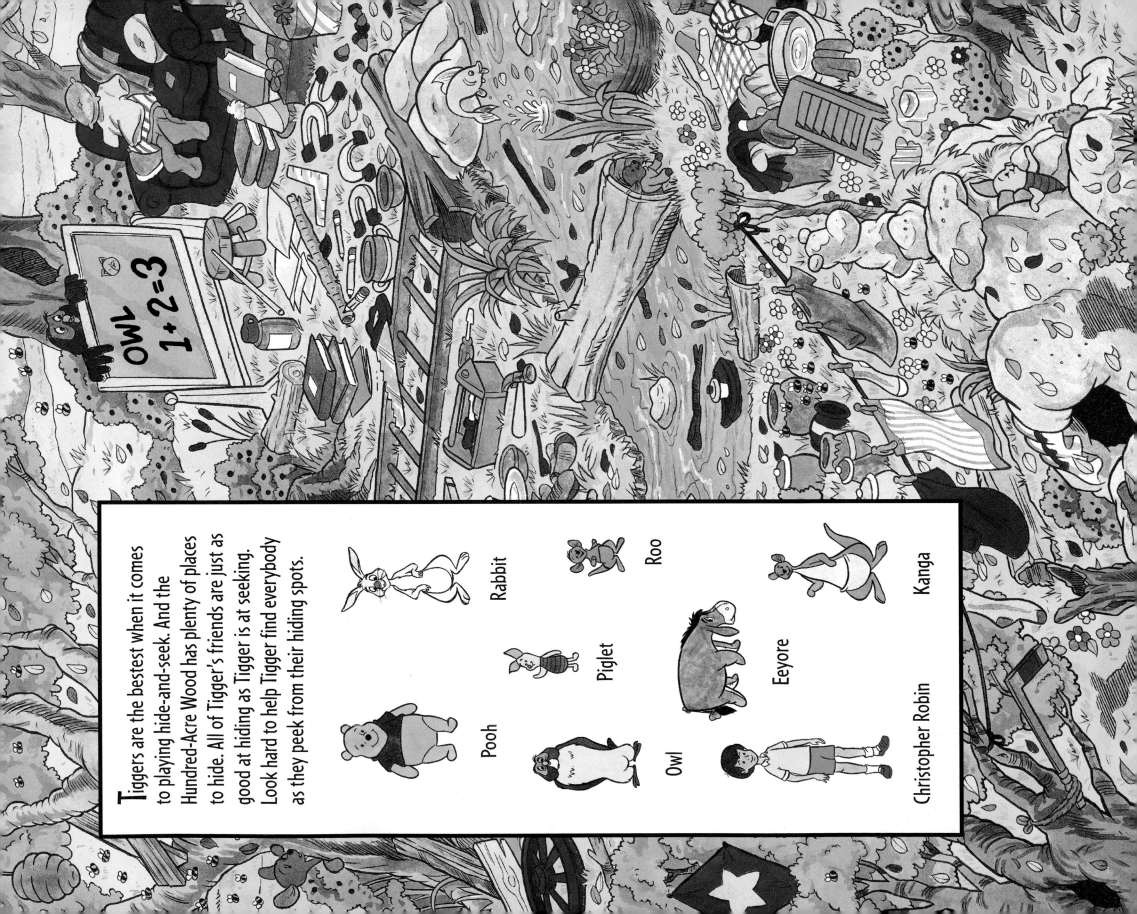

Tiggers are the bestest when it comes to playing hide-and-seek. And the Hundred-Acre Wood has plenty of places to hide. All of Tigger's friends are just as good at hiding as Tigger is at seeking. Look hard to help Tigger find everybody as they peek from their hiding spots.

Rabbit

Roo

Kanga

Piglet

Eeyore

Pooh

Owl

Christopher Robin

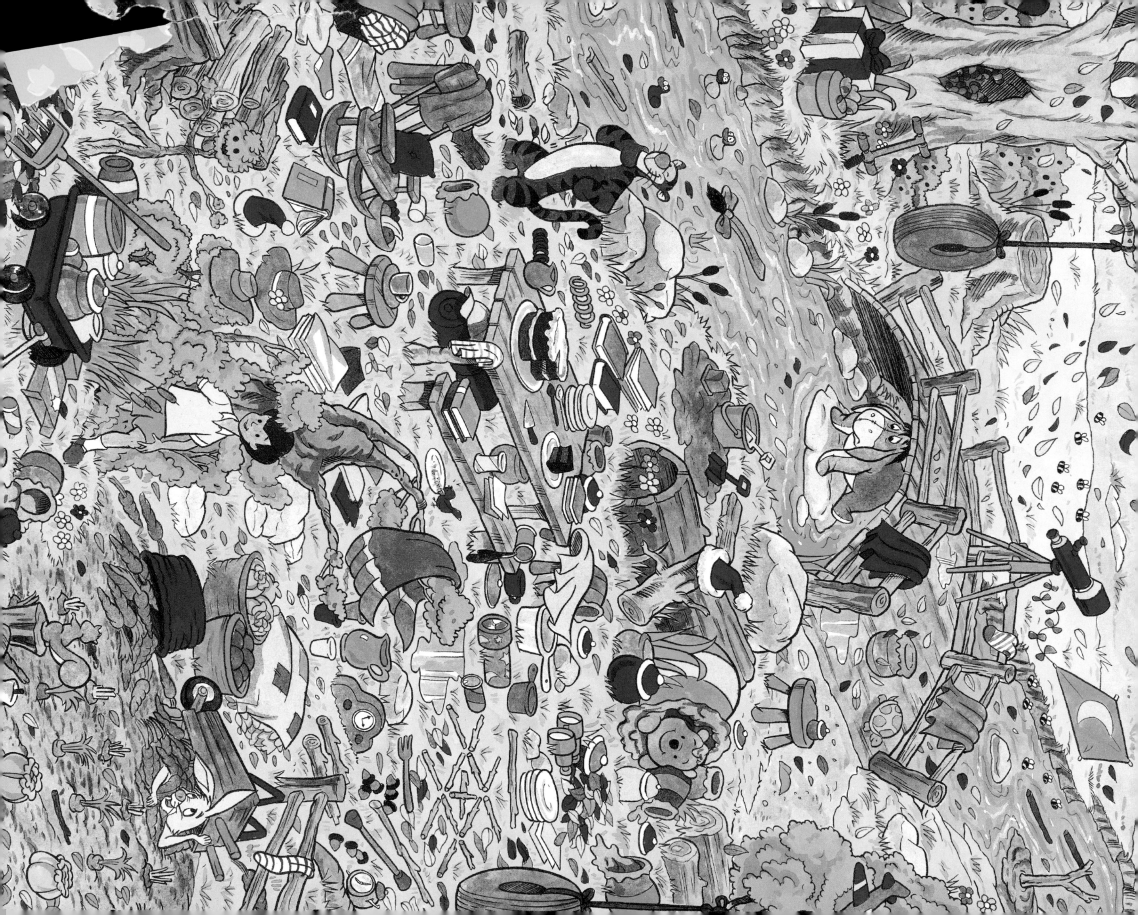

Tigger and his friends are starstruck! Can you find these other silly "stars"?

_____ Star Cookie
_____ Starfish
_____ Starflower
_____ Star "Dust"
_____ Star Dance
_____ Star "Light"

Owl certainly has a lot of friends and relations! Can you find these famous relations on Owl's wall?

_____ "Snowy" Owl
_____ Barn Owl
_____ Night Owl
_____ Great Horned Owl
_____ Wise Owl
_____ Owl and the Pussycat

Everything in Tigger's dream is so tiggery, and Tigger is having a hard time figuring out where everything is! Can you help him find these tiggerific things?

_____ Tigger Woods
_____ Tigger Lilies
_____ Candy "Striper"
_____ A Tiggery Baseball Glove
_____ A Tiggery Top Hat
_____ Tigger Bugs

When Tigger bounced-up Rabbit's garden, he also bounced-up all of Rabbit's gardening tools. Can you find these important tools so Rabbit can replant his garden?

_____ Hoe
_____ Rake
_____ Wheelbarrow
_____ Shovel
_____ Gloves
_____ Broom
_____ Watering Can

There are lots of fun things to do on a camping trip. Look for these things that will keep everyone, even bouncy Tigger, extra busy!

—— Hiking Boots
—— Guitar
—— Fishing Pole
—— Whistle
—— Compass
—— Hammock

It's such a blustery day that Tigger thinks he might be able to fly if he could just bounce high enough. Can you find these other high-flying objects?

—— Flying Butter Dish
—— Flying Carpet
—— Flying Dustpan
—— Flying Cup and Saucer
—— Flying Trapeze "Artist"

As soon as Tigger finds his friends, they're all going to play Pooh Sticks! Can you find these other fun "sticks"?

—— Stick Person
—— Stick-in-the-Mud
—— Measuring Stick
—— Pogo Stick
—— Hockey Stick

Before Pooh can clean up his house, he has to clean his cleaning supplies! Can you help Pooh find these things?

—— Broom
—— Dust Cloth
—— Sponge
—— Bucket
—— Mop
—— Soap